Here's Benjie!

Frances Walter • Violet T. Pearson

ACCENT BOOKS
Denver, Colorado

Second Printing, 1977
Third Printing, 1977
Fourth Printing, 1978

ACCENT BOOKS
A division of Accent-B/P Publications
12100 W. Sixth Avenue
P.O. Box 15337
Denver, Colorado 80215

Copyright © 1976 B/P Publications, Inc.
Printed in U.S.A.

Library of Congress Catalog Card Number: 76-50297

ISBN O-916406-60-1

Here's Benjie!

Meet Benjie

If you sit quietly beside a dam built in a stream, you might see a brown beaver swimming swiftly across the pool. Maybe it is one of Benjie Beaver's relatives.

Benjie is a young beaver. He lives with Mother and Father Beaver, his two sisters and one brother in their beaver pond. Father and Mother Beaver have built a beautiful beaver lodge in the pond for the family to live in. All the beaver kits helped. The beavers have a happy family life.

Benjie plays with his beaver brother and sisters much as boys and girls play together. They swim together. Sometimes they play tag together. Often they work together to find and prepare their food and to care for their home. When the young beavers disobey Father or Mother Beaver, they learn that it is better to obey. When they fight among themselves, they find out it is better to help each other.

Benjie and his family talk to each other in their own way. Of course, they do not talk as people do, but when we pretend that they talk, we can find out more about Benjie and his family.

Benjie's story shows us many things about the wonder of God's creation. We see that God made each animal in a special way to live in his own way. Benjie can't hop fast the way his friend Bunny Cottontail can hop. Bunny Cottontail can't thump his tail at the sign of danger and jump in the pond to escape the way Benjie can. Benjie learned to his sorrow that he cannot glide through the air like his friend Swifty the flying squirrel can. Chippy Chipmunk learned from his beaver friend that it could be fun to work.

Some animals can live near each other like friends. Other animals are natural enemies. Some animals are even food for other animals. Each creature of the woods has his own knowledge of what is danger for him and how to avoid it. In God's wisdom He made it to be so.

The Bible tells us that people are wonderfully made by God. The verse reads this way:

"I will praise thee [God]; for I am fearfully and wonderfully made. Marvelous are thy works, and that my soul knoweth right well" (Psalms 139:14).

This story about Benjie shows us that beavers and all the other animals are "fearfully and wonderfully made" by God, too.

As you read Benjie's story, you might want to watch for some of the wonders of God's creation.

Benjie Learns to Help

Benjie Beaver swam across the pond to the dam. He climbed up and sat down, looking all around him. The gentle breeze of early evening ruffled his brown fur. Father and Mother Beaver had worked hard to get the dam built to hold the water in the pond where they wanted to raise their family. Benjie and his brother and two sisters helped. There were always jobs for the young beavers to do to help the family get ready for winter. It was fun to help.

Benjie looked very small, sitting on the big dam. He breathed deeply of the cool fall air. He watched as the brightly colored leaves fell from the trees and tumbled into the water. They looked like little sailboats floating on the water toward the dam. There they stopped and made a pretty border along the dam. Benjie had a far-away, thoughtful look in his eyes.

"What are you doing?" asked Mother, as she swam up to him.

"I'm remembering when we were born," he answered, seriously.

His brother and sisters had come over and were listening to the conversation. "How can you remember when we were born?" asked his brother. "We were too little." Each of the beavers had climbed up on the dam by Benjie.

"I can remember just what Mother told us," replied Benjie. "Don't you remember she told us that a terrible flood came to the pond where she lived and washed away her family and lodge. She looked and looked for them, but could not find them. And it was time for us to be born." Benjie was very quiet and then asked, "Isn't that right, Mother?"

"Yes, that is right, Benjie," replied his mother. "I think that was the saddest time of my life. I had no home for you and I had no one to help me. I was very frightened. I had to have a safe place for you to be born, and a safe place for us all to live."

"You said we were born in a hollow by a fence," said Benjie, "but you didn't think it was a safe place for us."

"No, it wasn't," answered Mother. "A beaver is only safe when he has a home in the water. That is why we have a big lodge here in the pond that we can swim into. This way we can be safe and our enemies cannot get us."

"Did our first home look like this lodge?" asked one of the sisters.

"Oh, no!" exclaimed Mother. "Your first home was just a den in the bank of a stream. It was a hole some animal had dug out. I moved you there as soon as I could find it. I knew you could not get out of it, as tiny as you were, but I did not feel safe when I had to leave you to find food. An enemy could come along and find you. I knew I had to have a lodge to put you in."

"I know who built our first, big strong

lodge," said Benjie excitedly. "It was Father!"

"Is someone talking about me?" asked Father as he swam to the dam to join his family.

"Benjie is remembering," said Mother, moving over to make a place for him on the dam.

"That is better than forgetting," said Father. "But just what are you remembering, Benjie?"

"About when we were born and you were lost in the flood," replied Benjie. "Mother was telling us more about it."

Mother continued with the story. "When I put you in that den in the bank of the stream, I wondered how I could possibly care for you and build a dam and lodge all by myself. That is a lot of work, you know, for a mother beaver to do alone."

"Tell us," begged the young beavers.

"First, you have to find a good place on a stream for a dam. Then, the dam has to be built—"

"How?" asked Benjie.

His brother echoed, "Yes, tell us how."

"Oh, you funny kits," said their mother, "you know how a beaver builds a dam—"

"Tell us again, Mother," begged a sister beaver, nuzzling her nose into her mother's fur.

"Well," began Mother Beaver, "you know it is a lot of work. We have to get some rocks and logs together in the stream and pack them in real hard for a base, so the water won't carry them away."

"Don't forget," warned Benjie, importantly, "that we have to cut the trees first, to make the logs."

"Oh, yes, of course," answered Mother with a nod, "and that is where good beaver kits can help. Then we have to just build the dam by plastering more branches and logs and stones on the base until we get a dam built as high as we want it."

One of Benjie's sisters looked puzzled. "What is 'plastered'?"

As usual, Benjie thought he knew everything, so he answered before his mother could. "Why, that is putting the logs and sticks and rocks together with mud. Isn't it, Mother?"

"Yes, Benjie, you are right. Once we get the dam in place, the water in the stream begins to back up and we have a pond to live in and work in." She nodded her head toward their home in the pond. "We build our lodge where we live in much the same way."

"I know," said the sister beaver to show how well she understood her mother's explanation, "you built the lodge by plastering logs and branches together with mud. Am I right, Mother?"

"Yes, you have the right idea, dear." answered her mother. "You kits were so small then, I just didn't know how I was going to manage all this work and care for my babies, too. Then one day your father came swimming in the water near the den in the bank of the stream and my problems were all solved."

Father had been listening to Mother Beaver's story without making a sound. He had not heard the whole story before. They all turned and looked at Father, and Mother Beaver nudged him lovingly.

"You are a good father," said Benjie. "You made a new house for us."

"Yes, " Father continued the story, "I was carried far downstream in the flood. It took me many days to find where our pond had been. When I got there, everything was gone. Our lodge and dam were all swept away in the flood, and I could not find your mother or our family of beaver kits who were already half grown. I was worried because I knew your mother needed me."

"Oh, my," said a sister beaver, and they all listened hard for Father's next words.

"When I found your Mother," he continued, "she showed me where she had put you little kits when you were born."

Father agreed that it is good to think about things that have already happened and said, "That is all past but we must also think of things that are going to happen. The falling of the leaves and the crisp cool air are telling us that we just might be getting some cold weather soon. We have much to do to get ready for it. Who is going to help?"

"I will!" cried Benjie.

"I will!" cried each of the others in a chorus.

"Good!" Father said. "We have nice long nights to work. One of the many things we must do is to add to our feed pile. We must gather as much wood as we can and store it in the bottom of the pond, so we will have plenty to eat during the winter months." Father pointed toward a group of nice young trees as he talked. "When I was out inspecting the trees, I found a lot of the young trees still have too much sap in them to be stored."

"What is sap and what is to be stored?" asked Benjie completely bewildered.

Mother laughed and said, "Questions, questions. Benjie is a question box."

Father explained that the sap is a juice in the trees and to store means to put something in a good place so it can be used later. All of this was hard for such a young beaver to understand. Why put away the trees? All summer Father cut down trees and brought the young tender branches to the pond for them to eat so why put them away someplace?

Benjie still could not understand about the sap so he asked, "Father, why does the sap hurt the trees?"

"It doesn't hurt the trees," answered Father. "In fact trees must have sap to grow. But to store the trees, they can't have any sap."

Benjie still couldn't understand it all

but finally Father said, "Let's start by ringing the trees and you will soon know what it's all about."

"How can you put a ring on a tree?" Benjie wanted to know.

"You don't put it on," Father said laughing. "You have to cut a ring all around the tree. This will let the sap run out. Then in about a week, we can cut down the tree."

Benjie jumped up so excited that he almost fell off the dam. "Let's go ring around the trees," he cried and dived into the water. His brother and sisters followed him.

"Benjie," called Father quickly, "don't go on that bank until I get there!"

Benjie almost asked "Why?" Then he thought better of it. He and his brother and sisters played in the water.

Benjie swam by the shore and looked up on the bank. Why didn't Father want them to go up on the bank unless he was with them? Was there someone up there? Maybe someone was watching them?

Ring Around the Tree

All during the night the sound of the click, click of the beavers' strong teeth rang through the woods. Father had carefully checked for any enemies that might be hiding in the trees or in the shadows. Then he assigned each of the kits small trees close to the pond on which to work.

"You work right here," Father told them, "and I will go further into the forest." The beavers went right on with their work.

The whole family was busy cutting rings around the trees to let the sap run out. Next week they would cut down the trees and carry them to the water. There they would bury them deep on the bottom of the pond. How good they would taste if ice should cover the pond and the beavers could not get out to find other food.

"I've made two rings already," shouted Benjie.

"Let's see you do that big tree over

there," said one of his sisters, pointing to a larger tree.

"All right," said Benjie. "That won't take me long either." Benjie began to chip the bark off the bigger tree. He stood up on his hind feet and rested against his broad tail. He held on to the tree with his front paws. The bark came off easily. But Benjie just could not throw away all that good bark. He had to stop and eat a piece once in a while. All that work made him hungry!

Benjie was not really paying too much attention to what he was doing. He just kept chopping and eating. It seemed as though it was taking him a very long time to get around the tree. He wondered when he would meet the place he had started.

"Look at Benjie's tree!" his brother cried. The others came to look and they began to laugh.

"What is the matter with it?" asked Benjie, standing back to look at his work.

"Your ring is crooked!" one sister said as she walked around the tree. "You missed the starting place and you are

ringing two times in one." They were enjoying Benjie's funny-looking ring.

"What's so funny over here?" asked Father as he came to see what was going on.

"Benjie is playing ring around and around the tree," teased his brother.

"Did you get lost, Benjie?" asked Father

"Guess so!" said Benjie. He felt rather foolish but he thought it was funny, too.

"Oh, well, it doesn't hurt anything as the sap will run out of it just the same. That's a pretty big tree for such a little beaver. Are you planning on cutting it down or is that going to be my job?"

"I guess we were having a little race and I thought I could win even on this big tree," answered Benjie.

"I think you had better work on the smaller trees," replied Father.

Benjie just had to ask one more question. "What are we going to do when we finish this job?"

"Tell us, tell us!" the others cried together.

"Wait a minute! One job at a time," said Father. "Fixing the trees is the most important now. We need to do as many as we can before the sun comes up as we can't work in the daylight. Too many of our enemies would be able to see us and we would be in danger."

"Father," said Benjie, "you always talk about our enemies. Don't we have any friends?"

"Of course we do." Father laughed as he said, "We beavers are really very lovable creatures. Haven't you noticed how many ducks come to swim in our pond? Haven't you seen the turtles and the frogs climb on our lodge? There are many animals around that do not harm us."

Father was careful to watch the shadows in the forest as he talked. A beaver is never really safe on land as he cannot move very fast on the ground.

Father continued, "I only want you to be careful. One meeting with an enemy and that might be the end of you!"

"I will be careful," promised Benjie. "Did you ever meet an enemy, Father?"

"Oh, Benjie, you have more questions!" said Father. "Yes, I have met many enemies."

"But you are still here," said Benjie.

"Yes, and I am thankful!" Father answered. "I have had some terrible fights with enemies and had some narrow escapes."

The young beavers became very excited. "Tell us about them!"

"Not now," said Father. "We will never get our work done. No more talking now. Use your mouth for cutting that bark."

The beavers worked until the early light of dawn began to fill the sky and then they swam into their lodge and were soon ready for sleep.

Benjie asked his mother, "Do you know I have many friends?"

"You do? That is nice," replied a sleepy mother.

"Do you know why?"

"No, why?" asked Mother.

"Because I am so lovable!" replied Benjie.

"So you are," agreed Mother as she gave him a beaver hug.

It did not take the beavers long to fall asleep.

While the beavers were busy ringing their trees, two strange creatures were walking through the woods. These strange two-legged creatures were men. If Father Beaver had seen them he would have quickly called the young beavers into the pond and the safety of their lodge. Father Beaver knew that men were among his worst enemies. Sometimes men wanted the fur on beavers' bodies and would kill the beavers to get the fur.

The two men were walking through the woods when they saw the beaver dam and lodge in the pond. They stopped to look at them more carefully. Then they saw Father and the four beavers working on the trees.

"Let us stay here and watch them quietly," said one man. "I think we are far enough away so the beavers can't see us."

The other one nodded. "Or smell us," he added softly.

"I want to see inside of that lodge," said the first one.

"But how will you do that?" asked the other.

"When the beavers go in, I'm going to dive in the water and go up into the opening. Then I will be able to see just how they live inside their lodge," replied the first man.

So the men waited and watched the busy beavers all through the night. Finally one said, "They are all in the lodge now and have had time to get asleep. Are you really going to go in?"

"Yes, I am," replied the other.

Meeting in the Tunnel

The man waited a while longer to be sure the beavers were settled down for the day. Then he dived into the cold water. He soon found the tunnel that led to the lodge. Up, up he went. This man was not an enemy of beavers. He and his friend were scientists who studied about animals and how they lived. They wrote books about animals so people could learn more about them. This man knew that the tunnel would lead to a big room in the lodge. Once his head got in the lodge, there would be enough air for him to breathe.

But he forgot one important thing! A beaver's tunnel is made for beavers and not for men. He got part way up the tunnel and got stuck in a turn. He could not go forward. What should he do? He was in real danger. He could not hold his breath as long as a beaver. He must hurry and work to get out of the tunnel. He pushed and shoved trying to move his body.

The struggle woke Benjie.

"I wonder what all that noise is?" thought Benjie. "Can it be time to get up already? Maybe Father and Mother are out in the water. I'd better go see."

Half asleep, Benjie crawled into the main room. He did not see anything there so he decided to check around more. He dived into the tunnel and was swimming when he met the man face to face! If there had been room to jump, Benjie would have jumped very high with fright. Instead he smacked his little

tail and turned around and swam back into the lodge as fast as his little beaver feet would take him.

"Help, Father! Help, Mother!" he cried. "There is an enemy in our tunnel. He is a huge monster!"

The whole beaver family was quickly awake. They rushed out into the main room.

"Benjie, did you have a bad dream?" asked Mother.

"No, no!" cried Benjie. "A real enemy is in our tunnel. Go see, Father!"

The man was pushing and clawing and finally he worked himself back out of the tunnel. Quickly he surfaced and drew in deep breaths of fresh air.

Father swam out of the tunnel and to the surface just in time to see the man climb out of the water and up onto the bank of the pond. He knew Benjie was right. He could smell the scent of a man in the tunnel.

Father swam back into the lodge. "Benjie, you were right. You did see a real enemy, one of our worst enemies. I wonder why that man was trying to get into our lodge?"

"Could he really get into our lodge?" asked Mother.

"I don't see how he could," said Father. "Men are so much bigger than we are. I don't see how he got as far as he did. I am going to go out to see if he is still around."

"Oh, be careful," begged Benjie. "He is so big and fierce."

"Yes," agreed Mother, "do be very careful. He may want to kill us all."

"Benjie," said Father, "I want you to go with me, but you must be very quiet and stay right next to me."

Benjie and his father swam very quietly out of the tunnel. They hardly made a ripple in the water. They saw the two men walking away from the pond. If they could have understood human sounds, they would have known that the one man was making fun of the other and having a good laugh.

"So you found out you are not a beaver!" he said.

"Well, it might sound funny to you, but I was really worried," said the other. "I could have drowned."

"Did you see anything at all?" asked the man.

"It was very dark," said the other man, "but one of the beavers swam into the tunnel and saw me. He smacked a lot of water around. I knew he was going to warn the others, and I had to get out of there fast."

"You were under the water so long I was getting worried about you," said the man who had laughed.

"Well," answered the wet man, "no more trying to get into a beaver's lodge for me. Let's go. I want to get some dry clothes on."

Benjie and Father watched until the men were out of sight. Then they went back into the lodge.

"There were two men," Benjie announced to the others as he came into the lodge. "They have gone away now."

Father quickly added, "But we must be very careful. They know we are here and they may come back. We must stay in our lodge for at least another day."

"I don't think I ever want to go out again," said Benjie, and shuddered.

"Oh, yes you will," assured Mother. "You will go to sleep and soon forget all about it. Everyone back to bed!"

Benjie was just a little afraid but still very excited over this experience. He thought about it for awhile but was soon fast asleep once more.

Rabbits Are Different

The beavers stayed in their lodge and slept for a whole day and a night. The excitement had made them very tired. Father went out once to check the pond and the dam and found nothing. The scent of the men was gone. He knew the danger was over.

Benjie was the first to wake up. He stretched and shook himself until his fur was fluffy all over his little body.

"Benjie!" called his brother. "Are you trying to shake the whole lodge to pieces?"

"I am going to go find Father and ask him if all is safe," said Benjie. He could not find his parents in the lodge, so he knew they were out in the water. He hurried back to the bedroom as fast as his little legs would take him and shouted, "Let's go! Mother and Father are out in the water."

Mother and Father were slowly swimming in circles around the pond with their noses up in the air. The little

beavers came out of the lodge like torpe-
dos from a firing tube. One! Two! Three!
Four! Mother and Father turned in surprise as they watched each head pop up
out of the water.

"That is not the way to come out of the
lodge first thing in the evening," scolded
Mother.

"Why?" asked Benjie. "What other
way is there?"

"Mother means you should come out
quietly," explained Father. "A wise beaver always comes out very quietly,
swims slowly around the pond, and
smells for any signs of danger. That is

what Mother and I were doing when you all came shooting out of the lodge."

"Oh, I am sorry," said Benjie. "We will be quiet."

"It is not necessary now," said Mother. "There are no scents of enemies or danger around. You can make all the noise you want."

"Father, could you get me a nice piece of fir tree to make new bed chips?" asked Mother.

"Come on, Benjie," said Father, "let's go cut down a fir tree. You other kits stay and help Mother in the pond."

Benjie and Father went to the part of the woods where the fir trees grew. Father picked out a nice one and began to chip. Benjie used his little teeth to help, too. Before long Father said, "Go stand far away, Benjie. The tree is going to fall!"

Benjie hurried away and hid behind another big tree.

"Why are you hiding?" asked a soft little voice.

Benjie turned to see a little white rabbit. He looked so friendly that Benjie wasn't frightened at all. "I don't want the tree to hit me," he answered.

The rabbit seemed to think Benjie was quite funny. "A tree cannot walk. It will not hit anyone!"

"My father is cutting one down and it might hit me," replied Benjie.

"Why is he cutting down a tree?" asked the rabbit.

"We need it to sleep on," replied Benjie.

"Well, I never heard of such silly answers," said the rabbit. "How can you sleep on a tree?"

"I don't think I can tell you how. I could only show you," answered Benjie, wondering how he could show this little soft animal their beaver beds in the lodge in the pond. Could he swim to the lodge? "Who are you?"

"Oh, I am a rabbit. My name is Bunny Cottontail," answered the little animal in a small voice. Benjie decided rabbits must be beavers' friends.

"Where do you sleep?"

"Oh, we sleep in a hole in the ground, or maybe in a tree," answered the bunny, timidly.

That was a new idea to Benjie. "What do you mean, maybe you sleep in a tree?"

"Sometimes our mother finds a hole in a tree stump or in an old tree and makes our home there," the bunny answered.

"Our mother put us in a hole in the side of a stream once. That was when we were awfully little," said Benjie. "She called it a den, and she said it wasn't safe for us for very long. We beavers need to live in the water where we are safer from our enemies. Don't you have enemies?"

"Oh, yes, we have enemies," answered the little rabbit. "Lots of enemies and we are never really safe, not even in our beds in the hole. When we are in danger, we just have to hop real fast."

"Well, hop fast now," cried Benjie, and the bunny put back its ears and hopped away, just as the tree Father Beaver was cutting crashed to the ground.

"Benjie, come on," called Father. "It is safe now. Help me cut up the tree."

"I wonder if I will ever see that rabbit again," said Benjie. "I would like to be friends with him."

Working Together

As the weather got colder, the beaver family worked harder and faster. They seemed to know that it was necessary to get things done in case freezing weather should come. They needed to prepare a feed bed in the bottom of their pond for winter or for any sudden need for food.

Mother and Father did most of the heavy work. They cut down the trees and cut them up into smaller pieces. The little beavers rolled and pushed the smaller pieces to the water. Once the wood was in the water, it was easy to move. Father started the feed pile at the bottom of the pond. He forced a big strong tree into the mud and then added more around it. Back and forth they crisscrossed the wood and not one piece floated to the top.

"Benjie, you can carry these smaller pieces down to the feed pile," said Father. "Push the pieces in among the others so they will stay."

"Don't you think that work is too hard for that little beaver?" asked Mother, as

Benjie swam away.

"I don't expect him to do much," replied Father, "but it will be good practice for him. He will have to dive and come to the surface many times."

"What are the other little beavers to do?" asked Mother.

"They can help me bring the pieces to the water," answered Father.

Benjie was feeling very proud that his Father had given him this job to do. He took hold of a piece of wood with his strong teeth and dived to the bottom of the pond. He swam over to the feed pile and decided where to put the piece of wood. It was not a very big piece, but it would make a nice snack for a little beaver.

Benjie opened his mouth, but he forgot to hold the wood with his front legs. Up, up went the piece of wood.

"Come back, you wood!" called Benjie as he swam up after it. The water current was carrying it toward the dam and Benjie was swimming after it.

"Why are you playing tag with the wood?" called his brother.

"I'm not playing," replied Benjie. "I am working."

He grabbed the wood and took a firm hold on it once again. This time he held it with his front paws. Although it was hard for him, he managed to dive to the bottom with it. Once again he swam over to the feed pile. He pushed and grunted and finally got the piece wedged in between two other pieces. It did not come loose.

Benjie looked at his work proudly. Beavers can see under water. The Lord has provided them with "goggles" to wear. When they plunge into the water, thin transparent eyelids cover their eyes. This protects their eyes from dirt in the water and allows them to see.

Benjie came up out of the water. "I put my first piece down there, Father."

"Very good," replied Father, "but we have many more pieces waiting for you to take down. Do you want to try another?"

"Oh, yes," answered Benjie excitedly. He thought to himself that he would take a big piece this time so he could show Father what a good worker he was.

He chose a piece of wood that was just a little bigger than he was. He pushed it into the water. Then he guided it toward the middle of the pond where the feed pile was. He took hold of the piece of wood and tried to dive.

But the wood would not go down. It floated on the water. Benjie took hold of it with his teeth and tried to dive, but the wood just stayed on top of the water.

Now Benjie was really getting upset. He climbed upon the piece of wood and tried to push it down into the water. The wood rolled over and he fell into the water.

"Playing again, little brother?" called out Benjie's brother.

"No, I'm not playing!" exclaimed Benjie. "I am working very hard and this piece of wood just won't go down."

"Why don't you talk to it?" suggested Benjie's brother.

Benjie laughed and asked his brother, "Why don't you come to help me?"

"All right," said his brother. So the two of them worked and pulled and finally got the piece down. They shoved it into place.

"At last," puffed Benjie. "Thanks for helping. Now I am so hungry I could eat a piece just about that big."

"Please, please! Don't eat that one!" begged his brother.

"Don't worry. Not after all of that work," answered Benjie. "Let's go up for some food." And up the two hungry brothers went in search of food.

Making a Hiding Place

At last, the beaver family had finished their feed pile. Mother and Father knew they had enough food to last them if the winter should be long and cold, no matter how much Benjie ate.

"Well, we are finished!" exclaimed Benjie. "I think that is the most beautiful feed pile I have ever seen."

"But you have never seen one before," said his brother.

"Well, you are right," answered Benjie, "but I am sure it is the most delicious one."

"Yes, you can sure say that," replied his brother. "You took a sample of every piece!"

Just then Benjie saw Father and called out, "Father, you said we were going to do something else to get ready for winter. Can you tell us what it is, now that we are finished with the feed bed?"

"Yes, I can," replied Father, "and you will be able to help with this one, too. I want to make some refuge holes around our pond."

Benjie had a little beaver frown on his face. Father sometimes used words he did not understand. "What is a refuge?" he asked.

"A refuge is a safe place," explained Father.

"Oh, then we are going to make some holes safe," answered Benjie.

Father laughed. "Well, not exactly. You do have a way of turning words around, Benjie."

Benjie sat quietly and folded his front paws, ready to learn about refuges.

Father began to explain, "The refuge holes will be places of safety in the bank of the pond. We will start digging a tunnel in the bank of the pond several feet under the water, and then up, so we can make a small room above the level of the water."

Father was pointing this way and that, trying to help the kits understand his plan. "This way, if the winter is too hard we can swim into the refuges for a rest and they will give us a change from the main lodge. Or, if an enemy comes, it may give us a good, quick hiding place."

"Oh, that will be fun," said Benjie, happily. "I like to dig. Will Mother help?"

"Yes," answered Father. "She and your sisters can work on one tunnel and room, and we boys will work on another. It would be nice to have several, but we will see how the work goes."

Benjie, Father and the rest of the family swam around the pond and decided just where the refuge holes should be dug. Then Mother and the girls went to work on the opposite side of the pond from Benjie, his brother and Father.

Father began the opening under water, then he had the young beavers dig out the mud. This was easy work and Benjie loved to play in the mud and water.

"Look at me!" he called as he carried huge armfuls of mud out of the hole and dumped them in the water.

"You look like a mud pie," teased his brother, "and your hands are all dirty!"

"You can tease all you want," said Benjie. "But this work is fun. Think of the good times we can have swimming into these safe holes during the winter."

"Do all beavers make these refuge holes, Father?" asked Benjie.

"I don't know what other beavers do," replied Father. "But I suppose they do."

It did not take the beavers long to dig the tunnels for the refuge holes. Benjie loved to hurry in and out with his hands full of dirt. Each time he would bring it out, he had a good splash in the water. It seemed as though he made many, many trips.

As Benjie worked his way up into the tunnel, he heard an unfamiliar sound.

He was very quiet and listened. "Tap, tap, tap," went something above him. He hurried out of the tunnel.

"Father! Father! There is something in the tunnel making a funny sound," said Benjie. Father swam into the tunnel and the brothers followed. They all listened and heard, "Tap, tap, tap."

"What is it?" whispered Benjie.

"It sounds like something walking on the ground above us," explained Father, also whispering.

"Can it get us?" asked Benjie.

"I don't know," said Father. "I will swim up to see. You stay here."

Benjie wondered who had come to disturb them now? Was it an enemy?

Work Can Be Fun

As the brothers waited in the tunnel breathlessly, Father surfaced to the top. They could still hear the "tap, tap, tap" noise, and Benjie shivered.

"I hope Father is all right," he whispered to his brother.

"I do, too," answered the brother beaver.

"Listen," exclaimed Benjie, "was that Father's voice?"

Yes, it was. Faintly they heard, "Come out, boys, come and see what is making the sound that frightened you." Quickly the two little boy beavers surfaced to the top of the pond.

Benjie was the first to reach the top. "Where, where?" he cried. "What, what?"

His brother followed him with, "What is it, Father?"

"Look there, on the bank of the pond," said Father.

The two little beavers saw a large animal pawing the ground with its feet.

Each time a foot went down it made a strange noise, but it sounded different from the "tap, tap, tap" they had heard when they were under the ground, in the tunnel.

"It is just a lovely deer that has come to drink from our pond and to eat the moss," explained Father. "It is not one of our enemies. It will not hurt us at all."

"Oh, what a pretty animal!" exclaimed Benjie. "What long legs it has. I imagine it can run very fast on the ground."

"Yes, it can," said Father. "It must be able to in order to get away from its enemies."

"Does such a big animal have enemies, too?" asked Benjie's brother.

"Oh, yes," answered Father. All of us animals have enemies. The deer has some of the same enemies as we have. One is that man-creature who frightened you in the tunnel to the lodge, Benjie."

Benjie laughed as he remembered. "I guess I scared that man-enemy in the tunnel!"

The Father and two sons swam slowly in the pond, watching the deer as he drank from the pond and then walked off into the woods.

"I wish I had long legs like that deer," said Benjie.

Father laughed. "You would be a funny looking beaver if you had long legs. And you wouldn't be able to swim as fast, either."

"Oh, well, I will just keep my short legs then," said Benjie. "I would rather swim than run."

"You don't have a choice, you silly beaver," teased his brother.

"Maybe not," said Benjie, and seeing a good chance to play he gave his brother a big shove. He thought it was funny to see him tumble in the water. He kept shoving and shoving him even while he was trying to work.

Finally Benjie's brother got tired of it and said to Father, "Benjie is a shover."

"Oh, he is, is he?" said Father. "Well, I have a little surprise for him." He swam into the tunnel before Benjie could get out. Benjie had his hands full of dirt and was on his way out to dump it in the pond.

"Please let me pass, Father," said Benjie.

"Just go around me," answered Father.

"I can't," replied Benjie, "there isn't enough room."

"Oh, just give me a shove, then," suggested Father. Benjie pushed and shoved, but he could not move his big Father.

"I thought you were a shover," said Father seriously.

"I am only a little shover," said Benjie. "I can't make you move."

"Well, remember when you start to shove," said Father seriously, "there might be someone bigger than you that can shove harder and you just might get hurt."

"You're right, Father," answered Benjie. "I didn't mean any harm. I was only teasing."

Father nodded. "Let's go see how the girls and Mother are doing," he said. "It is time to go into the lodge anyway."

They swam over and found the others working hard on their tunnel. Benjie told the girls about the deer. They wanted to see it too, but Father said it was too light for beavers to be out. As they began to beg, Mother gave them a shove.

"Into the lodge, girls, as you were told," said Mother. "And you too!" Mother laughed as she gave Father a big shove. He pretended to tumble into the water.

Benjie acted very serious and said, "Oh, Mother, remember when you start shoving there might be someone bigger than you who can shove harder."

Father laughed and laughed. Mother looked wonderingly and Benjie giggled. Mother didn't know why Father laughed and how Benjie knew so much about shoving!

Benjie Learns About Snow

The beaver family finished digging the two refuge holes. Each had a nice wide tunnel leading to the hollowed-out rooms. Each room was just the right size for a beaver to rest in.

"Let's try them out," suggested Benjie. He and the other young kits took turns swimming in and out of the refuge holes.

"I like them!" said Benjie. "Maybe I will just live in one during the winter."

"I don't think it would be warm enough," said Mother. "You will want to stay in our big thick lodge if snow begins to fall."

"Why don't we go out in the snow?" asked Benjie. "I think that would be fun. I have a lot of nice thick fur on me."

"That is a good question," said Father, "and there is a good answer. Maybe you can discover it for yourself. Where is your fur?"

"Why, it is all over my body," answered Benjie.

"Over every single place?" asked

Father.

"I know one place where there isn't any," said Benjie's brother. "I don't have any on my tail."

"I don't have any on my feet," said one sister. Then the other sister added, "And I do not have any on my nose."

"Is that the answer?" asked Benjie.

Father nodded. "Yes, that is the answer," he said and then explained to the wide-eyed kits. "Our feet and tail would freeze very fast. We could only walk a little distance in the snow and then we would not be able to walk at all."

"There is really nothing on the snow covered ground for us anyway," said Mother. "That is why we make sure we have all our winter food down under the water before any snow falls."

"Do all beavers live where there is snow in the winter?" asked Benjie.

"There are many places where snow does not fall, and there could be beavers in some of these places," replied Father. "In fact, we do not always have snow here," he added.

Benjie's brother asked, "If the pond gets covered with ice, how could we get out to walk on the snow?"

"Sometimes it will snow before the water is all frozen," said Father. "If this should happen this year, you can stick your nose in it. And I think that will satisfy you. But it just doesn't feel as though it is going to be a very cold winter."

Mother suggested, "Right now I think we should have a good swim."

"Yes," agreed Father. "Soon it will be time to go to sleep."

"Let's play tag!" shouted Benjie.

"Don't you ever get tired of that game?" asked one sister.

"No, never, never!" cried Benjie. "Who can catch me?"

They dived in and out of the water. They swam to the dam and back.

Benjie began to swim around the lodge while the others chased after him. Then his brother thought of a good idea. He turned around and swam the other way toward Benjie. As Benjie came splashing around the lodge, his brother caught him.

"Ha, ha, I caught you!" shouted the brother.

"Hey! You played a good trick!" shouted Benjie.

"You only said we had to catch you," said the sisters as they swam up. "You didn't say how to do it."

Mother called out, "Sorry, no more time for games now. It is getting light and time for all little beavers to come in."

The little beavers quickly obeyed Mother and swam into the lodge. They liked to sleep, too. They liked to do just about everything! It was hard to decide what they liked to do the best. Benjie was sure it was eating, but then playing was fun, and there was the sleeping he enjoyed, and the working, too! He just knew that a beaver has the very best life of all!

Getting Cleaned Up

All the beavers sat on a ledge inside their lodge. It was a good place to clean themselves and eat their meals. The floor below them was wet with the water dripping from their fur as they came into the lodge.

Benjie listened while Mother taught the little beavers how to comb and clean their fur before going to bed. "Sister," said Mother to one of the girl beavers, "look how tangled your fur is. Use the two inside toenails on your hind foot to smooth it out."

"Like this?" the little one asked as she struggled to get her hind foot clear up to the tangle.

"Yes, you are doing fine. A little bit more and your fur will look nice again."

"I can scratch way up here with my back paw," said Benjie proudly. Then he proceeded to show the others how he could do it.

Then Father showed his little family how to sit on their tails and spread oil over their fur from an oil gland. "This will make your fur waterproof," he said. "You need to oil your fur often."

In order to reach the oil the beaver must sit on his tail. When Benjie first tried to sit on his tail, he rolled right over backwards. It looked so easy when Mother and Father did it.

"Are you having trouble, Benjie?" asked Mother.

"I can comb my fur all right, but when I try to get the oil, I just roll over," said Benjie.

"Well, just keep trying," suggested

Mother. "You will learn how after awhile."

Benjie was not the only one having trouble. The other kits were falling over, too. They had a good time laughing at one another.

"This is worse than Benjie's shoving," said the brother. "I can't blame anyone for my falling except myself."

As Benjie combed and combed his fur, he was trying to think of a way to sit so he wouldn't fall over. No matter what he tried, he could only sit that way for a few moments and his roly-poly body tumbled over.

"There must be a better way than this," mumbled Benjie to himself. "I always fall backwards. If I had my back against something I would not fall."

Benjie decided to back up to the wall of the lodge. There he sat on his tail and began to oil his fur. He did not fall after that.

"Look at me," said Benjie. "I am not falling now."

The others saw what Benjie had done. "What a good idea," they all said. Soon the other kits were sitting against the wall, too. It did not take them long to finish their combing and cleaning.

Mother and Father laughed at their four young beavers. They thought they were pretty clever to think up a way to keep from falling.

"It was really Benjie's idea," said Father to Mother. "He is going to grow up to be a fine beaver." Then Father said louder so all could hear, "How about a snack before we go to sleep?"

"Oh, yes!" cried the young beavers.

"Do we have to go out and get all wet again?" asked Benjie. "I have just finished drying and cleaning my fur. Don't I look lovely?"

"Indeed you all do look lovely," agreed their Mother.

"No, you won't have to go out," Father answered Benjie's question. "I have already brought in a piece of wood. Gather around and we will cut off the branches and have a tree feast."

Each beaver held his branch in his hands and began to turn it and chew off the bark. It looked as though they were eating corn on the cob. Click, click went all those sharp teeth, and in no time at all the bark was off the branches.

After they had finished eating, the young beavers were ready to go to sleep. Mother made sure they were all comfortable in their bedroom as they curled up close to each other. Soon each beaver was sound asleep, and Benjie had a dream about sitting up all night long on his tail and leaning back against the wall of the lodge.

An Enemy Scent!

The beaver family knew they would not be hungry if they should have a severe winter, or if an emergency should keep them inside the lodge for an extra long time. They had worked long and hard to make a big feed pile at the bottom of the pond. Many of the other animals did not prepare for winter months and they would get very hungry before the winter was over.

Out there, one of these animals, a wolverine, was hungry right now. Many of

the animals were already safe in their dens for the winter. Some sleep all winter and do not have to worry about food. But that does not help the wolverine any; in fact, it makes him even more desperate for food.

The beaver family at the pond was always so very careful and spent most of the time in the water so hungry wolverines didn't have much chance. If he could get one of them up on the land he could have a nice, delicious meal.

It was true that the beavers didn't go up on land much now. They had their trees all cut down, and their refuge holes were dug. They just kept repairing the dam and putting mud on their lodge to make it nice and strong. They really didn't have any reason to go on the land.

The next night as Father came quietly out of the lodge he began to scout around. He held his nose high above the water and took deep sniffs. His nose picked up the scent of a wolverine, so he swam back into the lodge to warn the others.

"Mother, do not let the kits go out tonight," he said. "I smell an enemy. I think it is a wolverine, and they are very dangerous for beavers."

Benjie was just coming into the room and heard what Father said. "A real, dangerous enemy?" asked Benjie in an excited voice.

"All enemies are dangerous, Benjie," said Father. "I do not want you kits to swim out at all tonight. Do you hear?"

"Oh, yes," said Benjie. "But how will we know what he looks like if we do not see him?"

"You don't need to see him," said Mother. "He is there. Father smelled his scent when he went out to scout."

"What are you going to do?" asked Benjie.

"Right now I am not going to do anything," answered Father. "I am hoping that he will go away. Then we will not have to worry."

"But I am hungry," complained Benjie.

"Well, I can dive down and bring up some food from the feed bed," said Father. "That will keep you busy, for a while anyway."

Father swam out of the lodge and surfaced long enough to once again smell the air. He dived down for a piece of wood and hurried back into the lodge.

"Did you see anything?" asked Benjie.

"No, but the scent is even stronger, and it seems to be coming from the direction of the dam," answered Father.

"Maybe some animal is just crossing over," said Mother. "They often do that. We don't mind if they use our dam for that."

"We will wait through this night, and if the scent isn't gone by tomorrow, we will know something is out there that is hungry and wants a beaver meal," said Father.

"Oh, dear, will he be able to get us?" asked Benjie.

"No, not as long as we stay in our lodge, he cannot get us," answered Mother. "You do not have to worry."

"After we finish eating, you kits can clean up your bedroom. This would be a good time to do this," said Father. "Then you can play some games."

"You can practice sitting on your tail, Benjie," said Mother. "That will keep you busy and give us all a good laugh."

The kits missed their usual swim and

play in the water, but they knew they were safe inside the lodge. They managed to keep busy and out of trouble, but all of them felt just a little bit uneasy. Benjie wondered what Father would do if the enemy did not go away.

Benjie Meets an Enemy

The next night Benjie asked to go out with his Father to check the pond, but Father said it would be better if he went alone. Then, if everything was all right, Benjie could go into the pond.

Father swam out very quietly into the pond and hardly made a ripple in the water. Only his nose could be seen above the water. He swam around and around the pond, sniffing for the scent of the enemy.

As Father swam back into the lodge, Benjie hurried to him, with the others following.

"Is it safe? Is the enemy gone? Can we go out? What is happening?" asked Benjie all in one breath.

"Please, one question at a time, Benjie," said Father as he laughed. Whenever Mother heard Father laugh, she knew everything was all right and could breathe a sigh of relief.

"I cannot smell anything tonight," said Father. "I guess the animal was just walking across the dam. We can go out in the water, but just to be sure, no one is to go up on the bank of the pond."

"Oh, goody!" said Benjie. "I want to swim and splash and dive and do all the things I can in the water before I forget how."

"Oh, Benjie," said Mother, "one night in the lodge is not going to make you forget how to swim."

"I don't know, Mother," said the brother in a teasing voice. "Benjie forgets very quickly."

Benjie answered his brother by laughing and said, "At least I am fast. Just try to catch me."

Out of the lodge shot the little beavers and a fast game of tag was underway. "Whew, I am glad they can go out and use up that energy," sighed Mother.

"I'll go out to make sure they don't get into any trouble," said Father. Father found the kits swimming around the pond as fast as they could. After they became tired of this game, they climbed up on the dam and dived off into the water.

"When you kits get through playing, you can put some more mud on the lodge," said Father.

"Where shall we get the mud?" asked Benjie.

"You can take more dirt out of the refuge holes, or from the bottom of the pond," answered Father.

"I am going to take mine from the bottom of the pond," said one sister.

"Me, too," said the other sister and their brother.

"I am going to take mine from the refuge hole," said Benjie, just to be different. The kits were so busy getting the mud and patting it on the lodge with their little paws, they forgot all about looking around for enemies.

Wolverines are very careful that they do not let the wind carry their scent to those they hope to catch for a meal. As the beavers played, a wolverine could be watching from where they could not smell him.

Several times Benjie came very near the edge of the pond as he swam to and from the refuge hole. He remembered that Father said they should not go up on the bank of the pond. He was careful to obey. He never went up on the bank.

But, the next time Benjie came up from the refuge hole, and passed near the

bank of the pond, he heard a great
S-P-L-A-S-H! Something grabbed him.
Benjie gave a cry of fear and began to
struggle with all his might. He knew
that the enemy wolverine Father had
smelled had him in his clutches.

"Father, Father!" he cried to himself.
"Come and help me!" But the animal
had him by the throat and Benjie could
not make a sound out loud.

The wolverine was pulling hard,
trying to drag Benjie out of the water.
Benjie fought to get loose so he could
dive. Oh, wouldn't someone help him?

Father Helps Out

Father was looking at the dam below water, to see if it needed any repairs. As he surfaced, he saw the struggle that was going on across the pond. One of his kits must be in trouble! He started swimming across the pond as fast as he could. The three young beavers followed.

"Everyone splash water at the wolverine," shouted Father. He began to smack his tail on the water, and the young kits did their best, too. The wolverine could not breathe or see with all that water splashing in his eyes and face. He dropped Benjie and tried to get away. But Father grabbed him by his neck and dragged him into the water. Benjie turned and sank his teeth into the tail of the wolverine and hung on tight. He was angry but frightened at the same time.

The wolverine struggled hard to get free. Father swam out into the pond with him. Benjie followed, still holding on to the animal's tail. Then Father dived down, down to the bottom of the pond with the wolverine.

Father could stay under for ten minutes or longer but the wolverine could not live that long under water and Father knew this. Benjie tried to stay under as long as Father, but he could not. He had to let loose of the tail and go up for air.

After what seemed a long, long time Father came up alone.

"Oh, Father, is he dead?" asked Benjie. "I am sorry I could not stay down any longer and help you."

"You did just fine, Benjie," said Father, and he hugged him tightly.

The sisters swam into the lodge to tell Mother what had happened. She quickly came out to inspect Benjie.

"Oh, Benjie, let me look at you. Are you

all right?" asked Mother.

"I am just fine," said Benjie. "I was afraid, but I was angry, too, to think that old enemy caught me."

"Benjie helped me drag the wolverine to the bottom of the pond," said Father proudly. "He is a good and strong fighter."

"Benjie is a brave brother," said his sisters.

"Yes, he is," agreed his brother.

Benjie said, "I really wasn't very smart to get caught like that."

"Let's all go down and see the wolverine at the bottom of the pond," said Father. "He will never hurt another animal again."

They all dived down and saw the enemy lying dead on the bottom of the pond. As they surfaced Benjie said, "What are we going to do with him? Shall we just leave him there?"

"No, I think not," said Father. "Let's drag him to the other side of the dam and the stream of water will carry him away."

It was easy to move the wolverine to the stream. He would soon be carried away, but Benjie would remember for a long time the narrow escape he had.

Father gave them some advice about fighting enemies. "If the enemy does not live in water, the best thing to do is to splash him with water and mud. This hurts his eyes and he cannot see well. While he is trying to get the water out of his eyes, try to drag him into the water. There you can drown him if you can hold him under long enough."

"What if you are fighting on land?" asked Benjie.

"That is very hard for a beaver to do," answered Father. "You have to be strong and try to use your teeth to break the enemy's neck or back."

"Have you ever fought an animal on land?" asked Benjie.

"Yes, I have." Father nodded thoughtfully. "I have fought them on land and in the water. But I can tell you, I do not like fighting at all."

"Neither do I," said Benjie. "It is too dangerous. I would rather make peace."

"You are so right, Benjie," said Mother, and she gave him another big beaver hug.

The Trick That Boomeranged

For many nights after the attack of the wolverine, the young beavers talked about enemies and just what they would do to them. They took turns being an enemy and the others tried to get them under water and hold them. Of course, it was only in play and no one got hurt.

"Let's see who can stay under the water the longest," said Benjie.

"Who is going to time us?" asked the brother.

"We will all dive in at the same time and when we come up, we will sit on the dam," explained Benjie. "The last one to come up will be the winner."

"That is a good idea," said the sisters. They all swam toward the dam. How the water splashed when they dived! None of them could stay down very long the first time. But the more they did it the longer they could stay.

Then Benjie had an idea for a trick. He decided that the next time he dived in he would go hide in a refuge hole, and the others would think he could stay down a long time.

Down they dived again, and off swam Benjie.

Benjie waited for what he thought was a long time and then swam out. He surfaced near the dam.

"I won!" he cried. Then to his surprise he did not see the other beavers around.

"What did you win, Benjie?" asked Mother as she swam over.

"I won a contest—I think," he said.

"I don't see any other beavers to be in a contest." Mother looked around. "If you were the only one in it, I am sure you must have won," she said, laughing softly.

"But I wasn't the only one," explained Benjie, puzzled. "Now where did those beavers go? They surely can't still be under water!"

"Why don't you look?" suggested Mother.

"I will, but if they are, then I did not win," said Benjie.

"I don't understand all the funny things you say," remarked Mother.

Benjie looked all over the pond, but he did not find the beavers. Then he looked in the lodge. They were not there, either.

"How did you lose them?" asked Mother.

"We were having a contest to see who could stay under the water the longest," explained Benjie. "I just played a little trick on them. I hid in the refuge hole and when I came out, they were gone."

"Maybe they did not like your trick," said Mother. "You were pretending to do something that you did not do."

"But wouldn't they know I was only playing a trick on them?" asked Benjie. "I play tricks all the time."

"Yes, you do," said Mother. "Still that doesn't make it right. Now you have no one to play with."

"Won't you help me look for them?" asked Benjie.

"I am sorry, I can't now," replied Mother. "I have work to do."

Benjie was feeling pretty lonely as he swam around the pond. "What I did really wasn't fair," he said to himself. "Maybe they swam far away and will never come back."

While Benjie was on the other side of the pond, his mother took matters into her own hands. She was sure she knew where the kits were, so she swam into the other refuge hole to look for them. There they were, all sleeping. "Say, little beavers, you'd better wake up," she said, pretending to scold. "You won't have any sleep left in you when it is time to go to bed." She gave each of them a beaver nudge with her nose.

The little beavers squealed and nuzzled their Mother. Then they all swam out into the pond.

Benjie shouted with joy when he saw them. "Hi, there! I am sorry I tricked you. I won't do it anymore."

"That's all right," said his brother.

"We came up out of the water and sat on the dam waiting for you . . ."

"And we were worried because you didn't come up, too," interrupted a sister beaver.

The other sister wanted to help tell the story. "We knew no beaver could stay under water so long. Not even Benjie."

"Then we knew you were up to your tricks again, Benjie," said his brother, chuckling. "So we decided we could fool you, too."

Benjie started laughing with the others. "I know now what you did," he said. "You all went to hide in the other refuge hole, didn't you?"

"Yes, we did," giggled a sister. "And we all went to sleep!"

"Come along, you little beavers," said Mother. "It is time to get to your work. Benjie is full of tricks and he will keep us laughing and happy all winter long."

Father said, "It looks as though the winter is going to be a mild one. That is good news."

Friendly Visitors

Mother and Father Beaver were working busily on their lodge. The four young kits were playing in the water nearby. Suddenly they heard a splash at the other end of the pool. Mother and Father thwacked their tails in alarm and the whole family dived for the bottom of the pool.

A beaver's tail not only helps him to swim, but it is used to signal danger. One of the first things a kit is taught is the use of his tail. He is taught to slap his tail on the water and then dive to the bottom. When Father slapped his wide, powerful tail down on the water with a loud thwack, all the kits knew this meant, "Danger! Dive at once!" They liked to practice slapping their tails and diving. It would be a long time before they could make a loud sound like Father and Mother did. They never stopped to ask "Why?" when the thwack rang out—they just obeyed and dived.

Now as the kits all waited at the bottom of the pool, Benjie shivered with excitement. He watched Father swim silently to the top and look around. Father's body jerked and he seemed angry. Then he called his family up to the top of the pool.

"The danger is over," Father told them, chuckling. "It's just that happy-go-lucky otter family. At first, I was very angry as I saw those five bodies going in and out of the water. I thought they were enemies. But the otters are friendly animals. You kits can go over and play with them."

Mother and Father went back to work. Benjie and the other beaver kits were so happy to see their visitors. They showed off their diving tricks. They showed the otters how clever they were at swimming under water. Then they all played a game of tag and a game of hide-and-seek. The otters could swim faster, and were best at water-wrestling, but the beavers could stay under water longer.

Just then Benjie thought of a new game. He swam over to the mound of sticks and mud that was the roof of his house. He got up on top and slid down the muddy slope into the water. Soon all the beavers and otters were on their tummies whizzing down the slippery mud slide of the lodge. It was such a messy game, but it was fun and they got washed off again each time they plunged into the water.

All too soon it began to get daylight and the otters swam off. Benjie thought it might be fun to swim off with them. But he decided to stay close to home.

Later, when he snuggled down into his nice soft chip bed to sleep, he was glad he had a good home and a safe place to stay with plenty to eat. The otters had to hunt their food and go to sleep in a new place every night. Benjie crept over a little closer to his brother and was soon fast asleep.

When Benjie Showed Off

"Benjamin!" called Mother. "You and your brother and sisters go to the shore and cut down some small trees."

"Yes, Mother," replied Benjie. He loved to use his strong orange-colored teeth to chisel into the trees and make them fall. The leaves and branches at the top were tender and delicious to eat.

"All of you stay close together and be very careful when the trees fall," warned Mother. The four beavers swam to the edge of the river and crawled onto the land. They began to look for the tall, slender cottonwood trees.

"Hello, Benjie," said a small voice. Benjie turned and saw that it was Bunny Cottontail. He was a nice little animal and Benjie didn't mind him being around. "What are you doing out of the water?" Bunny asked.

"I'm cutting a tree," Benjie said importantly. "Do you want to watch me? And you can ask me all the questions you want."

Benjie looked so clumsy that Bunny Cottontail couldn't help laughing. His tail was so queer looking, all covered with scales. It was so broad and flat. How could Benjie walk with it? "I am glad I have a little, fuzzy round tail," said Bunny. "It doesn't stop me from hopping quickly away."

"You can have your tail," answered Benjie a little sharply, "and I will keep mine, thank you."

"Benjie," exclaimed Bunny, "your hind feet look almost like those of a goose! And you have webs between your toes!"

"Why, yes," said Benjie, who didn't think they were queer at all. "My hind feet are for swimming. Look at my front ones. They look like little monkey hands. I use them to hold things and help build our dams and home. But I must hurry and find a good tree. Come, and I will show you what a good lumberman I am!"

Bunny Cottontail said nothing, but just hopped along beside Benjie, a little ways away from where the other beavers were busy cutting at the trees. Soon Benjie chose a nice little round tree. He stood on his hind feet, and using his big flat tail to brace himself, he put both hands on the trunk of the tree and went to work with his teeth. My, how those chips did fly! Bunny Cottontail saw how strong Benjie's teeth were. Before long the tree began to sway.

Benjie ran back for safety. He made a slap on the ground with his big tail to warn all the animals to run, so they wouldn't get caught under the falling tree. Bunny hopped far away, too, when he saw the beavers running. After the tree fell to the ground, the beavers went back to the trees they were working on. Bunny hopped back to sit beside Benjie and watch him work.

Benjie began to cut off all the branches of the tree. Next he cut up the trunk into small pieces. He ate a few of the tender leaves and branches, and offered some to Bunny Cottontail. But Bunny said, "No, thank you," and continued to watch. Benjie rolled or dragged the rest of the tree to the river. He showed Bunny that he wasn't so slow and clumsy after all.

"What are you going to do with all those logs and branches?" asked Bunny.

"We store the branches at the bottom of the pond for food and we use the logs to

build," explained Benjie. "Come on. I see
a nice big cottonwood up ahead."

Benjie wanted to show off for his
friend. He went farther away from the
shore of the river and the other beavers.

Bunny hopped with him for a ways.
When Benjie found a good tree he started
chiseling on it with his strong orange
teeth. Soon Bunny said, "I must be going
home. My Mother will worry about me.
Thank you for showing me what a good
lumberman you are."

"Come and see me again," called Benjie, as he watched the little ball of fur hop out of sight. Then Benjie looked around him. Nothing looked familiar to him. A strong wind was making a noise in the woods, but he didn't mind that. He was interested in the tree he found and wanted to finish his work on it. The wind became stronger. It blew the chips away as quickly as Benjie bit into the tree. And the wind was so noisy he didn't hear the crack of the tree as it began to fall. Before Benjie could run away, a jagged end of a broken branch went through his tail, and pinned him to the ground.

Benjie tried to run. He tried to jump. But the stick was stuck into the ground, and he couldn't move. What could he do?

Benjie Uses His Head

Oh, how Benjie's tail hurt! He called and called but no one heard him. He wished he had not gone so far from his brother and sisters. The wind was still blowing and making so much noise in the trees his small voice couldn't be heard from very far away.

He pulled and pulled until he was tired out. Then he sat quietly for a moment to rest and think. What would his father do if he were caught like this? Just thinking about his wise father made him feel better.

"Maybe I can cut the branch off," he thought. But he could not turn his fat, furry body so he could reach the branch pinning down his broad tail. "Oh, dear, whatever shall I do?" worried Benjie. When daylight comes, my enemies will come and eat me!"

Suddenly he noticed the ground where he was sitting seemed soft and sandy. With his front feet he started digging a hole. He scooped out the sandy soil on both sides of him as far back toward his tail as he could reach. He was almost standing on his head as the hole grew deeper. Finally the sand caved in, and the stick came loose. He was free!

Benjie hurried back to the pool and jumped in. How good the cool water felt on his sore tail! In time the wound would heal, but all the rest of his life Benjie would have a small hole in his tail to remind him not to be careless and a show-off.

Soon Benjie was back home and the rest of the family gathered around him.

They all wanted to know what had happened. Benjie was so ashamed that he had not obeyed. But he knew it was best to tell his family the truth. He loved his family too much to lie to them. So he told them all what had happened.

They all looked at the hole in his tail. Mother nuzzled him lovingly. Father said proudly, "That was good thinking, Benjie, the way you got loose."

His brother and sisters laughed at him and said, "Now when he slaps his tail, water will spray up like a fountain!" All the family laughed, but Benjie didn't think it was so funny.

"Come," said Father, "let's have a game of tag in the pool. Then we must gather up all the logs and branches that you busy beavers cut down."

Benjie soon forgot his sore tail, and had a grand time playing tag. He could catch his brother and sisters, but Mother and Father were much too fast for him.

Later, as Benjie got ready for a nice long sleep, his mother gave him a loving pat and said, "Benjie, I'm glad you are safe at home and all right."

"Thank you, Mother," answered Benjie. "I am glad, too. I'm going to remember to do as you and Father do. My ideas get me into trouble."

Benjie's Loving Mother

Mother Beaver came into the young beavers' room.

"Oh, hello, Mother," said Benjie. "Is it time to get up?"

"I just came in to see if you kits were all right," answered Mother Beaver. "Let me look at your injured tail, Benjie. Does it still hurt?"

They both examined the hole in Benjie's tail and decided it was healing nicely. "I almost think you are proud of that hole Benjamin Beaver!" Mother said, giving him a little shove.

"Well," answered Benjie, "it makes me different from all other beavers."

Mother looked around the room. "I want you to clean up your room, but you will need some new chips for your beds. You can use that piece of fir tree your father brought home."

"We will make some chips for you," said Benjie, speaking for his brother and sisters as well as himself, as he so often did.

"Let me show you how I can do it," and Benjie chewed away with his sharp orange teeth as one by one small chips fell to the floor. He didn't get choked on any splinters for special little folds of skin inside his mouth closed off his throat.

"Benjie, you're working backwards," scolded his brother. "You'll get the new chips mixed up with the old ones. Before you make new chips we should carry the old ones outside."

"Your brother is right," agreed Mother.

"But, Mother, before we do all this work please tell us the rest of the story about when we were born," begged the littlest sister.

"Please do," chimed in the rest of the little beavers.

"You will remember," began Mother, "that when it was time for you to be born, I had no home. I could not find the water. It was just beginning to get daylight, when I spotted a good hollow place by the fence. I went over and quickly shredded some bark and wood to make a soft bed in the hollow. I crawled into the nest and lay down there. That day you four kits were born. I was happy, but I had no one with whom to share my good news. Your father had been lost in the flood several days before."

Mother Beaver looked lovingly at each little beaver before continuing. "You kits slept in the warm soft bed I had made, but you were not protected from our enemies. I loved to nuzzle you, and brush your soft fluffy fur. You were each so small, and your little beaver tails were only a little bigger than my eye."

"And just look at them now," said Benjie's brother.

"Especially Benjie's," giggled one of the sisters.

Mother continued, "I was busy keeping you safe. You would have been a delicious meal for some other animal or bird."

They all shivered at the thought of being eaten and tried to get a little closer to their mother.

"As you grew more and more I knew I had to find water. A few little puddles from the flood were still around, but I could find no stream or lake. My fur was becoming dry and rough and you needed to be taught to swim. I wanted a den with an underwater entrance to keep you safe from our many enemies. One night after I fed you and you were fast asleep, I started down the dry stream bed to see if it would lead to water. I was sniffing as I went, for a beaver always has to be alert to danger."

Benjie moved toward his brother and sniffed, to show him how Mother had done.

"Suddenly I sniffed a strange smell—it was coming closer. I heard the twigs snapping, and I knew it must be a big creature. What could be the matter with him, that he was making so much noise? For creatures of the forest and plains have learned to travel quietly. What could this creature be?"

"Oh, tell us, Mother. What was it?" asked Benjie, sitting up in excitement.

"Why I . . . no I don't think I'll tell you until your work is done. Get busy, and do a good job."

"Oh, Mother," all the beaver kits sighed. But they knew she would keep her promise.

A Friend and an Enemy

Benjie and brother started to clean their room. The sister beavers helped too. Benjie filled his front paws with loose dirt from the floor. He went down the tunnel to carry it outside. Above the water, he looked around to check for danger. There on the edge of the pond was a strange animal sitting on a big rock. Benjie watched as the animal leaned over the rock and dipped his paws into the water. Benjie thought he looked like he was washing his face. Then Benjie saw him dip something into the water and put it in his mouth. Why, he was washing his food! Benjie looked down at his paws with the dirt from his room. Quickly he washed the dirt from his paws.

Benjie remembered that his father had told him about an animal who washed his food. He said that this animal had black rings around his eyes and a black ring around his tail. Father had said this animal would be friendly. Benjie looked.

His tail did have a black ring around it. Maybe he had found a new friend.

"Hello," called Benjie. "I'm Benjie. I'm going to call you Ring-Around-the-Tail."

"That's all right with me," said the animal. "I'm a raccoon. Would you beavers like to join me picking berries? I found a nice patch."

"We would love to," said Benjie for all the other beavers who had been watching and listening.

They were almost through eating the berries, when brother beaver said, "We were supposed to be cleaning our room. We forgot all about it. We had better run.

Thank you for showing us the berries, Ring-Around-the-Tail. They were good." So all the little beavers hurried back to clean their room.

Soon they had cleaned out all the old chips and made fresh new ones from the fir branch Father had brought to them.

"We are all through fixing our beds, Mother," said Benjie's brother. "Now tell us the rest of the story. What was this creature that made so much noise in the forest? Was it an enemy?" The beaver kits gathered close around their mother and looked up eagerly into her face.

"Yes, it was an enemy, a big strange enemy," said mother. "I could tell he was getting closer and closer. What if he came over to the hollow by the fence where I had put you kits? How could I protect you? I knew then that I must find a safe place by the water for you. Closer and closer came the noise of the twigs breaking. I had moved away from the nest in the hollow by the fence where you kits were sleeping. I didn't want this enemy to find you if he saw me. Suddenly he stepped out into a little clearing and I saw what it was."

"What did he look like?" asked Benjie's brother.

"What was he?" asked Benjie's brother.

"Ohhh!" squealed the two sister beavers.

"Just a minute," replied Mother. "One at a time, one at a time. He was tall, and he didn't have any fur. He had only two legs. He really looked odd. I recognized that he was a man and yet not a man. He must have been a man-child. Men are our greatest enemies."

"Why do men want to hurt us?" asked Benjie.

"They want our fur," answered Mother. "Men killed your father's cousins. I saw their skins with their beautiful brown fur. They were stretched out in front of a man's cabin. The four cousins were dead—all dead. We were so sad." Mother wiped away a tear.

"What did this creature do?" asked brother beaver.

"This man-child started straight for the hollow by the fence."

"Ohhh!" said the four beaver brothers and sisters.

"Quickly I got in front of him, and started another way. He followed close behind me. You know that beavers can't go very fast on land, but I went as fast as I could away from our beaver hollow."

Mother sounded excited as she talked.

"I thought that I now had him off the track, but suddenly he turned around and started right toward our temporary home. What would he do? Would he find you kits?"

"Did he find us? Did he kill us?" asked Benjie almost bursting with excitement.

"No," laughed his brother. "We wouldn't be here now if he had killed us, silly."

Mother bristled up her fur and looked much bigger. "This is what I did. I blocked the narrow path, and I hissed at him. He backed up, then, and ran back the way he had come. He never did see you little kits." And Mother Beaver nuzzled them. The beavers gathered close about her, glad that they had such a wise and loving mother.

A Joke Turned on Benjie

Benjie was a mischief maker and he loved to play tricks. He loved to thwack his tail and dive to the bottom of the pool even though there was no danger. Soon the other beavers caught on to this trick of his.

Sometimes he would creep up behind his brother and sisters as they sat on the bank and push them into the water. They would be so surprised they would slap their tails and dive. When they came back up, Benjie would be sitting on the banks swaying back and forth in beaver laughter.

Benjie thought this would be a good trick to play on his big lovable father. So one day while Father Beaver sat quietly eating a piece of bark, Benjie leaped on his broad tail. In a flash the big beaver flipped his tail and tossed Benjie into the air. Father then shot into the water, gave his tail a mighty thwack and dived to the bottom of the pool.

Benjie was a little surprised at the

somersault he had made in the air, but he sat down on the bank and waited for his father to come up and share the joke with him.

He waited and waited. But Father did not come up.

Benjie began to get scared. He dived into the pool and saw his father lying on the bottom of the pond! Benjie nudged him, but he did not move.

Benjie swam to the top of the pool and thwacked his tail. His brother and sisters paid no attention. They thought he was playing another trick. He swam to them and told them about Father. They hurried to the bottom of the pond and, sure enough, there was Father lying on the bottom of the pond—not moving at all. They all tried to move him, but couldn't.

Finally all the young beavers swam for Mother who was in the lodge. "Oh, hurry, Mother!" begged Benjie. "Something terrible has happened to Father. He has been on the bottom of the pool for a long time!"

"And he doesn't move!" added his brother.

As they all swam to the place where they had left Father they heard a tremendous slap of a beaver tail. They all jumped with fright and dived to the bottom. When they carefully came up, they saw father, who had come to the surface behind them.

They all gathered around Father and clung tightly to him. Benjie hid his head in his father's fur and promised never to scare anyone again.

Father Beaver then showed them many beaver tricks for hiding and remaining under water. Beavers can stay under water for long periods. He showed them how to make this seem longer by going up to the surface of the water without a ripple to take a deep breath of air and go back down.

Soon the beavers were practicing to see who could stay under the longest. Benjie's sister always won. She was so quiet and calm. This helped her to lie on the bottom of the pool for a long time.

As Benjie went to sleep that day, he thought again of his trick and how he was so frightened that something had happened to Father. He loved his father very much and would never do any thing to harm him.

Benjie Shows a Friend
How to Work

Benjie found a tall, straight tree and had just begun to cut into it with his sharp teeth when he heard a voice cry, "Don't you dare! Don't you dare cut down that tree!"

Benjie slapped his tail and jumped. Looking around he saw a tiny little red-brown animal with black stripes down

his back. He was coming out from the trunk of a big tree behind Benjie. It was Chippy Chipmunk.

"Now, don't tell me you live in this tree," laughed Benjie. "It is too small for even little you."

"No, I don't live in it," replied Chippy. "I live in a hole under that big tree. But this tall straight tree you were going to cut down is my safety post. I run up it every morning to see what is going on and see if any of my enemies are around. Even if it is not very big around, it is very tall. I run clear up to the top in no time at all!"

"All right," said Benjie. "I won't cut down your safety post tree. There are plenty of others."

"Why do you beavers always have to cut down so many trees?" asked Chippy.

"We use them for food, to build our homes, and for dams, and to keep our teeth sharp," explained Benjie.

"You go to a lot of trouble to make a home. You beavers surely work hard. Tell me how you make your house," Chippy said.

Benjie laughed. "Our work is fun and

useful. We hardly think of it as work because we have so much fun doing it. We start at the bottom of the pool. That's fun right there, diving in and out of the water. We take down brush and branches and pile them at the bottom. We cement them together with mud and stones. I can carry stones with my front paws," Benjie said proudly. "Soon the pile is so high it is above the water and looks like an island. Across the bottom it is almost twenty feet wide."

Chippy was listening to every word.

"And we keep piling and cementing until it is six or seven feet above the water," continued Benjie. "After this is done, we dive to the bottom and dig water runways or halls into the lodge, as we call it. We make at least four halls so we can all leave quickly—or scramble in quickly—if an enemy comes."

"Oh, my!" exclaimed the tiny chipmunk.

"In the very center of this big island we chisel out a large room," continued Benjie. "Here we eat our food and dry our fur. Then we fix our bedrooms. We never sleep with our Father and Mother. They have a room, and my brother and sisters and I have a room. We make our beds of soft chips. That is why we cut so much wood."

"Oh," said Chippy and started to leave, but stopped as Benjie eagerly kept on with his story about his home.

"We keep building and adding to the lodge to make it very thick so no enemy can get into it. We don't like messy beds, so we cut new chips often and throw the old ones away. We beavers are neat and very proud of our homes. That is why work seems like play."

"You make me tired thinking of all that work," yawned Chippy. "I'm going back to my tree and sleep." And with a flip of his tail, he disappeared.

"It is a good thing *beavers* are not lazy," thought Benjie, as he gnawed away at a tree, "or all our work *would* seem like work and too hard to do!"

Benjie Faces Danger

Benjie climbed onto the bank and pressed the water from his fur with his small paws. His mother had taught him how important it was to clean and comb his fur.

He remembered that mother had said, "If you stay in the water too long your fur will become too wet. The second toe on your hind foot has a special split claw made just for combing water from your thick fur. When you clean and comb your fur the oil from little sacs on your body put oil all over your fur."

Benjie was careful to keep his fur dry and oily. He was glad he could water-proof it any time he needed to.

After Benjie was well-combed, he realized how hungry he was. He made his way into the forest to find some tender branches and maybe some berries. Who was that coming? Why, it was his friend Cottontail, and another little bunny named Fluffytail hopping along.

"Where are you going, Benjie?" asked

Cottontail. "My, how clean you look."

"Oh, thank you," replied Benjie. "I just combed and oiled my fur. I'm going to look for berries."

"Good," said Cottontail, "so are we. Let's all go together."

Before long, Fluffytail hopped on ahead.

"Don't go so fast, Fluffytail," called Cottontail. "Let's stay with Benjie because he can't go as fast as we can on land." But Fluffytail kept right on hopping fast.

"Thank you, Cottontail," said Benjie. "But I could beat you bunnies in the water."

"I guess you could," said Cottontail, hopping slowly beside Benjie. "We bunnies can't swim at all."

Cottontail looked at Benjie again carefully. "You mean you comb your own fur and oil it?" he asked. "You can do many wonderful things. My fur grows thicker in the winter and then, as warm weather comes, it falls out so I won't be too warm."

Benjie was glad Cottontail had come along. He was good company and could find berries very quickly.

Suddenly a most horrible cry rang through the forest. Cottontail jumped. Benjie slapped his tail.

"What was that?"

"Oh, oh," said Cottontail. "That is Hooter the Owl. He is after Fluffytail. Why didn't he stay with us?"

Then they saw Hooter dive at Fluffytail ready to seize him.

"Fluffy, Fluffy!" called Cottontail. "Follow me!" And off they ran into the forest.

Poor Benjie couldn't hope to keep up with Cottontail. He flattened himself against a rock until he looked almost as if he were part of it. He hardly breathed as Hooter flew right over him and sat on a branch of a tree nearby.

"I don't dare move," thought Benjie. "I know owls won't attack big beavers, but I don't think I'm big enough for him to leave me alone."

Hooter stared and stared with his big owl eyes at the lump on the rock. Benjie wished he were bigger. He was glad he knew how to stay very still.

Then Benjie heard another hoot from far away. Hooter began to hoot in answer and flew away to find the other owl.

Benjie ran as fast as his beaver legs would take him to the pool. He jumped in and swam for the lodge. Not until he was in his own room, did he let out a long breath. Now he knew he was safe.

Why Benjie Can't Fly

Benjie stayed around the lodge and the pool for many days. He couldn't forget how frightened he had been by Hooter the Owl. He didn't want to meet up with him again.

He helped his family add more mud and sticks to the lodge. The thicker it became the safer they all would be. He also helped his father check the dam and fix any places that looked weak. If the dam broke, the water would leak out of the pool. It takes a lot of work and time to build a new dam. Beavers are very careful to check the dam often and work on it constantly. It is the first thing they build when they make a new lodge. The dam must be very strong to stop the flow of water to form a pond. A beaver's work is never done!

One night Father Beaver said he was going to the fir forest to get some new wood for their beds.

"May I go?" begged Benjie. He had

never been to the fir forest and he knew he would be safe with his big father.

"Why, yes, Benjie," replied Father Beaver. "I think that would be a good idea. I can show you where the fir forest is and then you will be able to go by yourself the next time. I want to leave right away. It is a long trip for our short legs."

"I am ready to go," said Benjie and with that he scooted out of the lodge into the water. Father was right behind him.

It was far into the night when they reached the fir forest. It was very deep and dark, and so quiet that Benjie couldn't help feeling a little afraid. He stayed close to his father.

"Here is a nice tree," said Father. "You start chiseling on this one. I am going to cut on that one over there."

"Don't go too far away," said Benjie. "I don't want to get lost."

"No, I won't," promised his father. "But if you need me just thump your tail, and I will come."

Benjie watched his father waddle away, and then began to cut on the fir. It would make a nice soft chip bed.

As he worked he thought he heard a

rustle in the leaves overhead. He stood very still for a moment and looked up. Then he saw it. A little creature was softly gliding from one tree to another. Then suddenly there were dozens of them flying through the air and playing like children. Benjie was fascinated as he watched them. One of them came down and sat on a stump near him.

"Hello," said Benjie. "What kind of a creature are you? I have never been to the fir forest before, and I have never seen anyone like you."

"I am called a flying squirrel," said the little creature in a small, soft voice. "But my friends call me Swifty because I can glide so fast."

"How can you fly so fast without making any noise?" asked Benjie.

"Oh," laughed Swifty, "we don't really fly. We just run to the top limb of a tree, give a big jump and come gliding down. I have a big fold of skin between my front and hind legs on each side. When I jump, I stretch my legs out flat and that forms a blanket and helps me glide. My tail helps me keep my balance and I can steer with it."

"How come you are out tonight?"

asked Benjie.

"We only play at nighttime. We stay in our hollow tree home during the day. We like it best when it is windy and stormy out. Then we can really sail." Then he ran up the tree and glided from one tree to another until he was out of sight.

Benjie watched Swifty go and sighed. "I wish I could fly like that. Wouldn't it be wonderful to glide through the air from tree to tree?"

Then he saw a tree that had fallen against another, and he got an idea. He would try to fly! Very carefully he walked up the fallen tree. It really wasn't very far off the ground, but it would do for a start. He took a big breath and jumped off. He tried to spread his legs out. Kerplunk! He landed right on his tummy, and nearly knocked the breath out of him.

"Whatever are you doing, Benjie?" called Father, who had been watching him.

Benjie had a silly look on his face as he said, "I was trying to fly like the flying squirrels."

Father laughed and said, "What a

funny Benjie I have! Which would you rather do, fly from tree to tree, or swim in the cool pond?"

"Oh, the pond is ever so much better," replied Benjie. "There are many tricks you can do in the water."

"Well, then let us forget about flying," said Father. "Those flying squirrels were made for flying from tree to tree, so that is what they do. You were made for the water, and that is where we are going."

Father helped Benjie up and the two of them dragged the piece of fir wood toward the lodge.

"No flying squirrel could do this," said Benjie.

"And he couldn't cut chips or build a home in a nice cool pool of water," agreed Father.

"I am glad I am a beaver, after all," said Benjie.

A Friendly "Boom-Boom"

"Time to get up," called Father Beaver, as he stuck his head through the tunnel into the young beavers' bedroom. They were huddled close together and still asleep. "I guess those new fir chips are just too comfortable. You don't know when to wake up."

Benjie yawned. "That was hard work dragging the wood back to the lodge and then chipping it up," he said. "And I am so hungry."

"Come on," called Mother. "We have some tender leaves and bark waiting for us on the bank of the pool."

The beavers all tumbled out of the tunnel into the water. Beavers are in the water so much they don't have to worry about dirty hands and faces or ears! Father had cut down a small tree, and it was a nice meal for them all.

"Father and I are going to check the dam tonight," Mother told them. "We want you beavers to go and cut down some small trees and bring them over. That way we can repair any place in the dam where it is weak."

Benjie, and his brother and sisters went off into the woods. They laughed and tumbled along. Benjie kept trying to step on his sister's tail, but she always managed to move it just in time. It was a game they never tired of playing.

"I choose this tree," called his brother.

The others moved further away to find trees. If they worked too close together, a tree might fall and hit one of them. Benjie had a hole in his tail to remind him how much a fallen tree can hurt.

Benjie's sister had just begun to cut a

tree when she heard a sound that frightened her. It began slowly at first and then faster and louder, "Boom-boom, boom-boom."

She went over by her sister. "Did you hear that?"

Her sister answered in a whisper, "Yes, what was it? I thought it was thunder."

Their brother came over, "Did you hear that sound that sounded like a drum?" The three huddled together. They were too frightened to move. They called to Benjie with thumps of their tails.

Benjie hurried over. "What is the matter?" he asked.

"Did you hear that awful sound?" they asked.

Benjie laughed right out. "Don't you know what that is? Father told me about that sound when we were out together." Benjie didn't mention the fact that he too had been very frightened and had clung to his father. "That is nothing but the sound of a ruffled grouse. He is a good friend of ours. Come, I'll introduce you."

The beavers made their way toward the boom-boom, boom-boom sound.

Benjie called out so the bird wouldn't fly away. "Drummer, come meet my brother and sisters." Drummer was sitting on a log.

"Why, he looks just like a fluffy ball of feathers," exclaimed a sister beaver. They all gasped with pleasure as Drummer spread out his tail until it looked like an open fan above his neck. It had broad bands of black and gray. Around his neck was a big ruff of black feathers.

"Show them how you make that sound," asked Benjie.

Drummer dropped his fan tail and began moving his wings up and down, first slowly, and then faster. That is the way he made the thunder sound. Then he flew over to a bush.

"Isn't that wonderful?" asked Benjie.

"Yes, but you can make a loud sound with your tail on land and water," said Drummer. "I know that means danger when I hear it. I thought there was danger tonight because I heard tails thumping."

"Oh, that was my sisters calling me," Benjie laughed. "They were frightened of your sound. We both frightened each other with our sounds!"

"Make the drum sound again," begged the beavers. Drummer did. Then Benjie slapped his tail. Soon they were all making sounds and laughing. It sounded like very noisy animal music.

Father Beaver heard it down at the dam and came to see what was going on. He had to laugh, too, when he saw the beavers all thumping their tails in time with Drummer's boom-boom, boom-boom.

But Drummer flew off into the night when he saw big Father Beaver coming. The other beavers went back to cutting down the trees. The forest was full of wonderful and friendly creatures, and they were glad they could have fun together.

Benjie Learns to Obey

Mother and Father Beaver watched their young beavers splash and play tag in the water. The sisters squealed with delight whenever they could catch their brothers. Benjie tried to tag his sister, but she always managed to dive to the bottom of the pond just as he was about to touch her. He would slap his tail and dive after her. Soon they got tired of playing this game and decided they would try to find some pond lily roots. These roots grew deep into the water, and were delicious food for the beavers.

The four beavers swam along under the water near the bank of the pond, but found no pond lily roots.

"Let's go further down stream," suggested Benjie.

"All right," said the others, "but remember what Father said about going too far away from home."

"Oh, we are still at home. We are in our stream, aren't we?" asked Benjie.

Away they swam from the lodge, down

the stream. They would dive under the water and swim as long as they could, looking for roots. Then they would come up for a little air, and go down again.

Benjie thought the others were too slow and swam on ahead. He came to another pond, and there on the edge were delicious roots. He began to eat them. Beavers can eat food under water. They have little folds of skin over their teeth so the water doesn't get in their lungs. Benjie was eating away, when he heard something move behind him. He thought it was his brother or sisters.

"Say, these are good. Have some," he said.

"What are you doing in my pond?" said a gruff voice. Benjie whirled around and there was a beaver almost as big as his father.

"Oh, sir, I didn't know this was your pond. I was only looking for lily roots. I live upstream," explained Benjie.

"You'd better get out of here, or I am going to give you a good beating," growled the big beaver. He reached out his hands to grab Benjie. Benjie slapped his tail and swam as fast as he could back upstream. He didn't bother to turn

124

around to see if the beaver was following him.

"Benjie," called his brother and sisters as he swam by. "Where are you going?"

"Come on! Come on home, fast! A big beaver is after us," called Benjie.

They all turned and swam as fast as they could after him. They never said a word until they were safe in the lodge. Then they sat and panted and panted to catch their breath.

"What is the matter with you kits?" asked Mother. "You act as if something had frightened you."

"A big beaver," panted Benjie. "He tried to get me."

"Ho, ho," said Father. "You went into another beaver's property. You know the law of the beavers. Each family is to stay in its own pond and not to bother others. Would you like it if all kinds of beavers came into our pond and lodge? Of course not. You have seen me walk around our pond and drop castors. This is to let other beavers know that this is my pond and home."

Beavers have a special little sac of oil near their tail. They drop castors or drops of oil around their property. The castors have a strong smell. When other beavers smell this, they know they are not welcome. They never go to another beaver's home. Father Beaver made his rounds often, and laid fresh castors. He wanted to make sure that no one would come and bother his family.

"I was in the water and couldn't smell anything," said Benjie. "I don't see why he had to be so gruff."

"Well, he didn't know if you were an enemy or not," answered Father. "You were wrong in going into his pond. He has never bothered us. But if he did come up, I would chase him away. You ought to be glad he didn't give you a good thrashing. If you had been bigger, he would have."

"For once I am glad I am not so big," said Benjie. "One time I want to be big and other times I want to be little. I guess I will just have to be the size I am."

Mother Beaver laughed. "Yes, Benjie, I am afraid you will. But never fear, you are growing stronger and wiser every day!"

"I am wise enough now to know I had better obey my Father and Mother and the beaver laws," said Benjie.

His brother and sisters snuggled up beside him. "We are, too," said his brother.

The two little sisters nodded and giggled.

Watch for more
books in the
continuing story of
Benjie Beaver.